T is for tuatara

Amazing animals from A to Z

Crazy critters with feathers or scales
Some with claws, and many with tails
Some make you smile
Some fill you with dread
Beginning with A and ending with Z

Written by Jo van Dam
Illustrated by Deborah Hinde

PictureBook Publishing

Aa – aardvark

The aardvark is a funny old mix,
A critter made out of leftover bits.
Ears like a rabbit, pointed and big.
A very long tongue and a snout like a pig.
Its feet are webbed, with bear-like claws,

An unusual sight! You stop, you pause.
This isn't a lie, I promise it's true –
Its tail is like that of a kangaroo!
It loves to eat insects, from holes it has dug,
Thinks termites and ants are the tastiest bugs.

Aardvarks might look like a mix of pigs, rabbits and kangaroos, but one of their closest living relatives is the elephant. Aardvarks can eat 50,000 ants and termites in one night.

Bb – blobfish

Gobby Bobby blobfish, goodness gracious me!
You are extremely ugly, that's clear for all to see.
It seems that you've been voted, the ugliest beast there is.
I think perhaps you are — you're a frightful, freaky fish.

Your nose is strange and droopy, your eyes are round and odd,
You mooch around the ocean floor; frankly you're a slob.
Gobby Bobby blobfish, goodness gracious me ...
It's lucky Bella blobfish, thinks you're cute as cute can be.

The blobfish spends its time blobbing around in very deep water, close to the seafloor. It opens its mouth when it sees something to eat floating past. In 2013, the blobfish was voted 'The World's Ugliest Animal' which is a bit mean. When it is deep under water it looks like a normal fish, but when it's dragged to the surface, its body can't handle the change in pressure, and it turns into an ugly blob! Poor misunderstood blobfish!

Cc – chameleon

Kim the chameleon's a camouflage star.
She can hide in a tree, she can hide in a car.
But her best trick of all is at birthday parties,
When she hides in plain sight in a bowl full of Smarties.

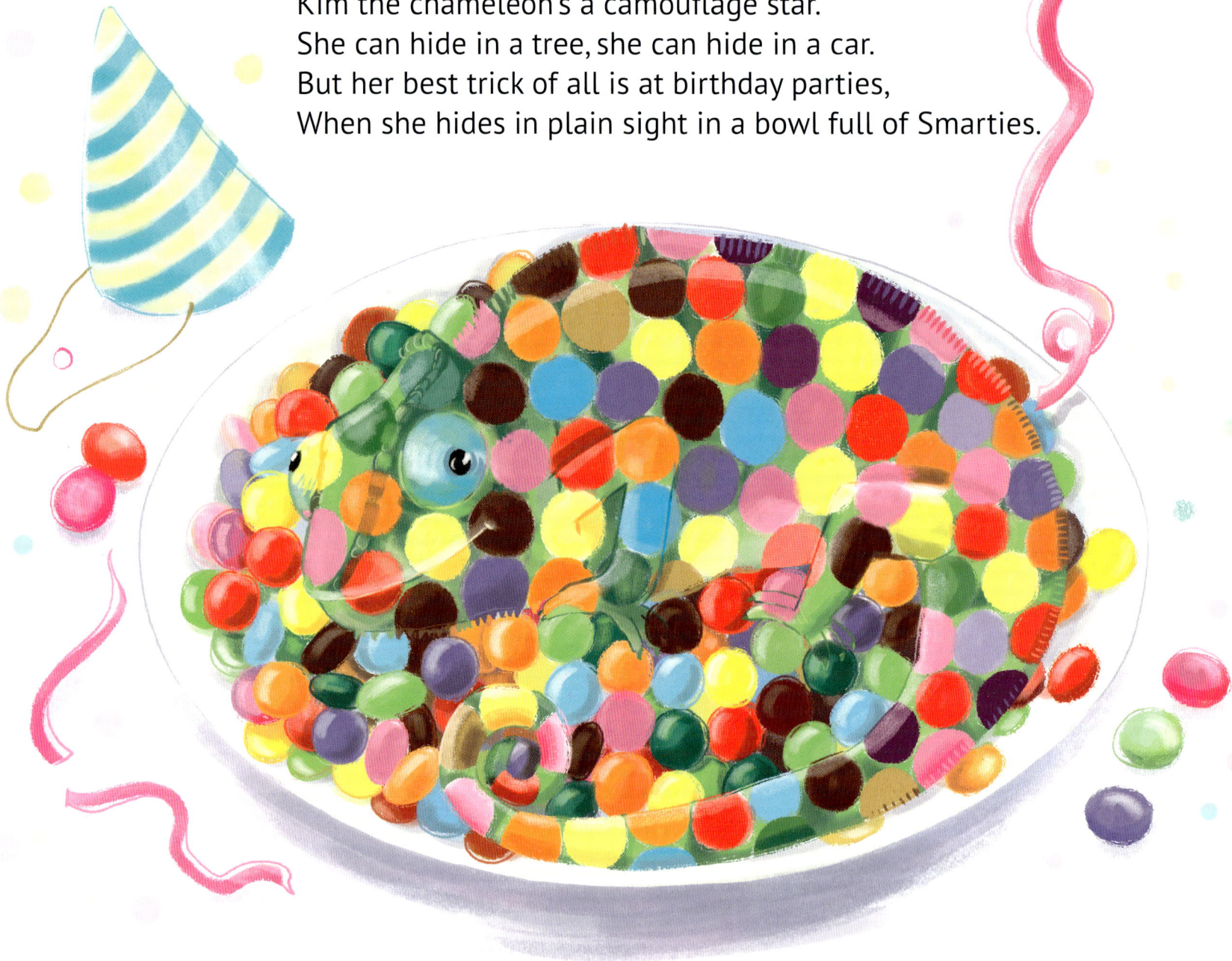

Chameleons have amazing eyes that can spin round and look in two different directions at the same time. They are also one of the few creatures in the world that can change the colour of their skin. Some chameleons can create patterns of pink, blue, red, orange, green, black, brown, yellow and purple.

Dd – dugong

Say gidday to a dugong called Kyle,
Who always wears a great big smile.
On sea grass he munches
For breakfast and lunches
A grin on his face all the while.

A dugong is a vegetarian, and it eats only sea grass, chomping through nearly 40kg every day. It has a flat tail and flippers like a whale, but its closest relative is an elephant.

Ee – emu

urrk!

There once was an emu named Eve,
Who dined on small reptiles and leaves.
She swallowed a lizard
Which stuck in her gizzard
Now Eve prefers fruit, bark and seeds.

Nom nom!

Emus are omnivores and eat bark, shoots, fruit, leaves, flowers, insects, seeds and small reptiles.

Ff – flamingo

Phil the flamingo loves to dance,
in shallow lakes, he'll strut and prance.

Phil the flamingo is very pink,
Because of things in the water he drinks.

Phil the flamingo stands up to nap.
On just one leg …
What a clever chap!

Z ZZ ZZ …

Flamingoes are born with grey feathers, but turn pink because of carotenoid pigments found in their diet of blue-green algae and brine shrimp. Flamingoes are well known for their dancing skills.

Gg – gharial

The gharial is lurking in the murky, muddy river.
If you spy his fearsome fangs, it's sure to make you shiver.
His teeth, as sharp as razors, could nibble off your toes.
But I bet you have a giggle when you see his funny nose.

Ha ha ha ...

The jaws of the gharial are very slender and long and contain 110 extremely sharp teeth. An adult male gharial has a large bulbous blobby growth on the end of its snout.

Hh – hedgehog

snuffle ... snort

Quickly prickly hedgehog,
A dog is on the run!
Quickly prickly hedgehog,
It's looking for some fun!
Quickly prickly hedgehog,
It spots you by the wall!
Quickly prickly hedgehog,
Roll into a ball!

When a hedgehog is frightened it rolls into a ball, hiding its head, tummy, feet and legs in a prickly coat of sharp spines.

Ii – indri

I love you Izzy indri
Your eyes so round and bright.
Your fur is soft and fluffy
Jet black and snowy white.

I love you Izzy indri
Your tail is barely there.
You are so cute and cuddly
Just like my teddy bear.

Indris are one of the largest species of lemur in the world, but unlike other lemurs, they have a very short tail. They spend most of their time in the treetops. Their button-like eyes and rounded ears make them look like teddy bears.

Jj – jellyfish

Squishy squashy jellyfish,
In the sea so green.
Wibbly wobbly jellyfish,
With tentacles so mean.
Blibby blobby jellyfish,
Swaying with the sea.
Stinging stunning jellyfish,
Please stay away from me!

The sea wasp box jellyfish is the deadliest jellyfish in the world. It has 15 tentacles, each up to 3 metres in length. Each tentacle has approximately half a million darts and each dart could kill up to 60 people.

Kk – kiwi

There once was a kiwi called Rob,
Who found some worms under a log.
But Rob was unlucky
The worms tasted yucky
That poor hungry kiwi called Rob.

Kiwi can't see very well but the nostrils on the end of their beaks make them very good at smelling things. Kiwi have tiny wings, but they can't fly. They have no tail feathers, but have whiskers, like a cat.

Ll – llama

Lou the llama is in disgrace,
Can you guess what she has done?
She spat at her owner; got him right in the face,
And spit in your eyes isn't fun ...

Pffft!

Llamas spit if they are annoyed with another llama ... or person.

Mm – mandrill

The mandrill wears a coat of grey,
Gold hair upon his head.
His bottom is bright red and blue
His nose bright blue and red.

The mandrill is a colourful chap,
Who likes to pose and strut.
He is not considered a pretty beast,
As his face looks just like his butt.

*Male mandrills are the largest
monkeys in the world. Just like
us, each mandrill has its own
fingerprints. Their bottoms are
certainly unusual and very
colourful, but luckily other
mandrills quite like a
colourful bottom.*

Nn – numbat

Meet a shy little numbat called Riki,
Whose tongue is long and quite sticky.
Termites get captured
And Riki's enraptured
'Cause termites taste yummy to Riki.

Mmmm ...

Sigh ...

Numbats have a thin and sticky tongue, 10–11 cm long. For a smallish creature, that is a very long tongue. They dip them into narrow gaps in the ground and wood to collect termites. Termites are the only thing they eat!

Oo – ocelot

Lottie is an ocelot,
A stripy, dotty ocelot,
Swimming in the lake a lot,
The sun had made her boiling hot.

Dipping in and out a lot.
First she's hot, and then she's not ...

So now she is a snotty-lot,
A sniffly, snuffly, sneeze-a-lot,
A cranky, croaky, cough-a-lot
Poor Lottie's caught a cold!

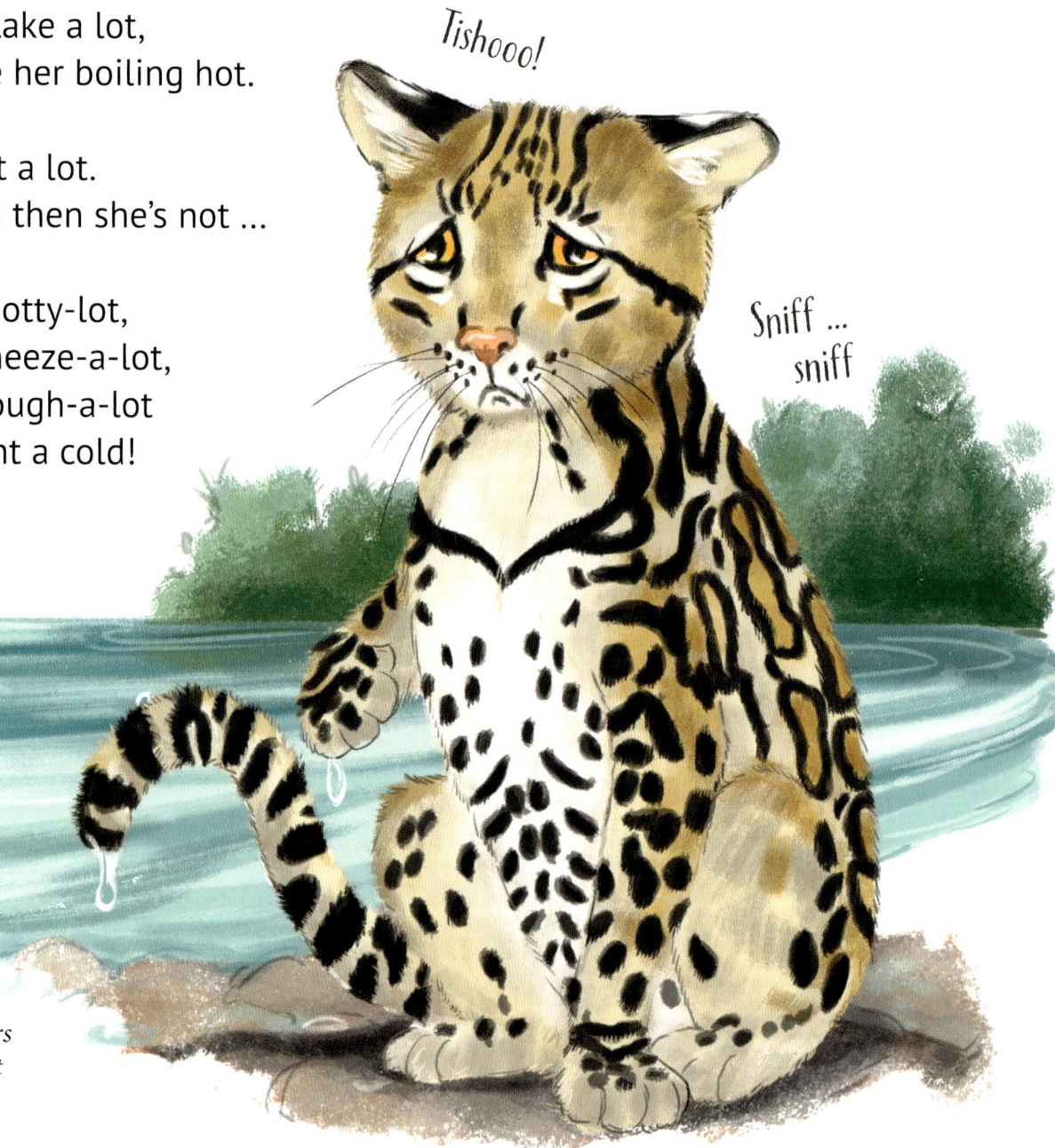

Tishooo!

*Sniff ...
sniff*

*Ocelots are very good climbers
and jumpers, but unlike most
other wild cats, they are also
very strong swimmers.*

Pp – piranha

Piranhas are South American freshwater fish with razor-sharp teeth. Not all piranhas eat meat, some are vegetarian … but others eat everything … even their own families!

Pip the piranha is ever so sad,
She can't seem to find any friends.
It's because when she meets them,
They think she might eat them.
And she might …
Pip just ate her Dad!

Qq – quail

Quail are small, plump birds. They can fly short distances, but you usually see them walking. A plume of black feathers sits on the top of their heads, bobbing and wobbling as they walk.

One quail, two quail, three quail, lots.
Can you count their odd topknots?
Four quail, five quail, six quail, more.
Can you find all twenty-four?

Rr – rhinoceros

Munch munch …

The rhinoceros loves to gobble up leaves.
He likes to nibble on bushes and trees.
He's not at all fussy, eats grasses and twigs.
It's amazing that veges can make him so big!

The name rhinoceros comes from the Greek word rhinocerōs meaning 'nose horn'. Black rhinoceros can weigh over 1,300 kg … and all they eat are plants!

Ss - skunk

There once was a skunk called Ding Dong,
Who smelled very bad, very strong.
But he wasn't to blame
All skunks smell the same
And other skunks quite like his pong.

pong

Sniff

Skunks are one of the top five smelliest animals in the world.

Tt – tuatara

Tuatara Tia has a birthday in a week,
She's turning ninety-seven, so her friends have planned a feast.
Beetle buns and spider rolls, and other tasty treats,
A cake with slugs and bugs and grubs, and all her favourite meats.
Just the sort of birthday cake a tuatara eats,
But ... ninety-seven candles will put out a lot of heat!

Tuatara look like lizards but are actually the last member of the order Rhynchocephalia. They have been around for over 200 million years. Tuatara can live for more than 100 years and have a third eye.

Uu – umbrellabird

Let it drizzle
Let it pour,
Umbrellabird
Loves nothing more.
Bring on rain
Bring on showers,
Umbrellabird
Stays dry for hours.

Umbrellabird
Has a bright red chest,
He looks absurd
With his crazy crest.
But umbrellabird
Is a lucky fella,
That crazy crest
Makes a great umbrella!

Splish ...

Splosh!

Umbrellabirds are big black birds with a funky hairdo that looks a bit like an umbrella. The male bare-necked umbrellabird has a red patch of skin on his throat. All umbrellabirds have strange, dangly wattles, some bigger than others.

Vv – vultures

Vultures like meat,
That is stenchy and rotten.
The leftover bits,
That a lion's forgotten.

They clean up the plains,
They're not at all picky,
They eat up the food,
That most think is icky.

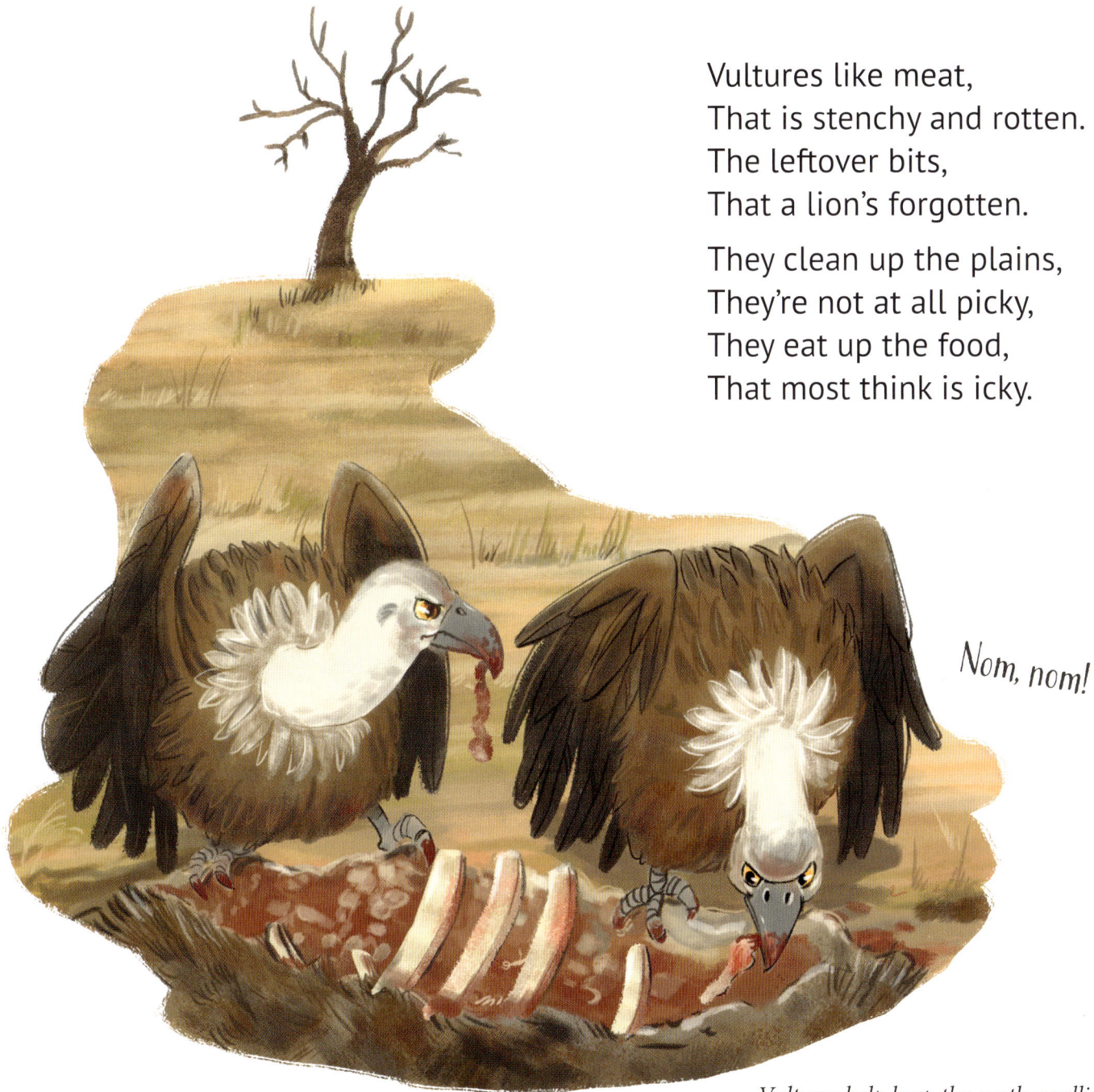

Nom, nom!

Vultures help keep the earth smelling sweet! They eat animals that have died. If the vultures didn't eat them the animals would rot, and smell revolting. If you ate rotten meat you would be very ill, but vultures have strong immune systems, so they do just fine.

Ww – Wētā

Have you ever met a wētā?

Would you like to pet a wētā?

Write a letter to a wētā?

Make a trap and net a wētā?

Or maybe better for the wētā ...

Leave the wētā quite alone.

Wētā are considered the dinosaurs of the insect world, having been in New Zealand since prehistoric times. They may not be pretty but they are unique, and we need to protect them and stop them from becoming extinct.

Xx – x-ray tetra

X-ray tetra,
Her name is Petra,
In the tank she hides.
But we can see you, Petra dear,
At least, we can see your insides ...

X-Ray Tetras are transparent – you can see right through them.

Yy – yellow-eyed penguin

Most people think
That penguins are cute.

Like very small humans
Dressed up in a suit.

They waddle and doddle
Right down to the shore.

Then waltz in the waves
With a swoop and a soar.

The Māori name for yellow-eyed penguins is
hoiho, which means 'noise shouter', because they
have a very loud call.
Yellow-eyed penguins are one of the rarest and
most ancient species of penguin in the world.

Zz – zebu

Stinky!

Pong!

There's a terrible smell at the old waterhole,
The zebu have come for a drink.
They should probably swim
As the stench is quite grim
But being so large, they might sink!

Zebu secrete a smelly substance to keep insects away, and like other types of cattle, they don't find it easy to swim.

Let's learn a little more about these amazing animals!

Aardvarks live in dry habitats throughout Sub-Saharan Africa. The name Aardvark means 'earth pig' or 'ground pig'. Aardvarks are nocturnal animals and eat ants, termites and sometimes African cucumbers.
What is the first word in the English dictionary?

Blobfish live at depths of 1,000 metres or so in waters around Australia and New Zealand. They don't have much bone or muscle, so the deep-sea pressure helps provide support for their bodies. They eat passing crabs, mollusks and sea urchins.
What colour are blobfish eggs?

Chameleons live in the warm rainforests and deserts of Africa, as well as parts of Europe and southern India. There are 160 species of chameleon; the smallest is 15 millimetres long and the largest 69 centimetres. Almost half of the species live in Madagascar.
Find Madagascar on a map.

Dugongs live amongst and graze on sea grass in the shallow coastal waters of the Pacific and Indian Oceans, and around east Africa; the largest population is in northern Australia. Dugongs breathe in oxygen and can hold their breath for up to 11 minutes.
Do dugongs grow tusks?

Emus are endemic to Australia and are the second largest bird in the world. The male emu incubates the eggs, never leaving the nest to eat or poo. They use their small wings for steering while running at speeds of over 40 kilometres per hour.
What colour are emu eggs?

Flamingoes are wading birds. There are four species distributed throughout the Americas, and the Caribbean, and two species are native to Africa, Asia, and Europe. Their backward bending 'knee' is really their ankle; the knee is further up the leg.
What is the collective noun for flamingos?

Gharials are critically endangered. They live in river habitats in Nepal and northern India. The gharial is a fish eater but will also eat other medium-sized aquatic animals like frogs and insects. *What do you think has caused gharial numbers to reduce?*

Hedgehogs can be found across Europe, the Middle East, Africa, Central Asia and Austalasia. There are 17 species. A hedgehog has around 6,000 spines on its body. Each spine lasts about a year before it drops off and a new one grows. A group of hedgehogs is called a 'prickle'.
What is a baby hedgehog called?

Indris are only found in the eastern parts of Madagascar in lowland jungles and rainforests. They spend their life in the trees moving from branch to branch. They can leap 10 metres! Indris are diurnal and eat the fruit, leaves and flowers of trees.
What does diurnal mean?

Jellyfish Sea wasp box jellyfish are extremely venomous with long poisonous tentacles. Unlike other jellyfish, which just float around, box jellyfish can swim, and they can also see! They have clusters of eyes on each side of the box. Fancy a swim anyone?
How fast can a sea wasp box jellyfish swim?

Kiwi are found only in New Zealand and are the only bird on the planet with nostrils at the end of their beaks. A kiwi will moult throughout the year as its feathers are more like hair than feathers. They can run as fast as a human!
Can you name the five species of kiwi?

Llamas are native to South America, but can now be found all over the world. Llamas speak to each other by humming. Llamas and alpacas are often confused, but the best way to tell them apart is by the shape of their ears. Llamas ears are banana shaped!
What are baby llamas called?

Mandrills live in rainforests of equatorial Africa. They live mainly on the forest floor, but move into the trees to sleep. Mandrills live in groups called 'troops' or 'hordes'. Their diet consists of meat and vegetables. *What word describes animals that eat meat and vegetables?*

Numbats are an endangered marsupial now only found in small numbers in Western Australia. Numbats are diurnal so seek shelter in hollow logs at night. They only eat termites.
How do numbats differ from other marsupial?

Ocelots can be found in Central America, from as far north as Texas and as far south as Argentina. The ocelot is about twice the size as of an average housecat. A female ocelot is called a 'queen'.
What is a male ocelot called?

Piranhas live in the rivers and lakes of South America. Piranhas have a single row of razor sharp teeth that interlock. Their bottom jaw has an underbite. The word piranha translates to 'tooth fish' in the Brazilian Topí language.
What is an underbite?

Quail California quail are ground-dwelling birds that live in coastal scrub land throughout California. Quail can also be found in other parts of the world. They eat seeds and grains along with fruits, nuts and insects.
What is the collective noun for a group of quail?

Rhinoceros There are five species of rhinoceros: two African and three Asian. Rhino horns are made of the same protein that forms our hair and nails. Rhinos love to have a mud coat – it keeps them cool and insect free, and gets rid of parasites. A group of rhinos is called a 'crash'!
What is a parasite?

Skunks are nocturnal animals the size of housecats. Skunks have a special weapon! They have scent glands on their butt that can shoot a stream of super stinky sulphur spray more than 2 metres to scare off predators. People have been known to smell skunk spray from 1.5 kilometres away! *What are baby skunks called?*

Tuatara are only found in New Zealand. Tuatara range from olive greens to browns to orange-red and can change colour over their lifetime. Tuatara have a crest of spines running down their neck and along their back.
Can tuatara grow a new tail?

Umbrellabirds live in the in mid to upper storey of tall trees in the rainforests of Central and South America. There are only three species and all are classed as vulnerable.They're not good at flying, so they hop from branch to branch. Umbrellabirds eat fruit and small animals.
What is a male umbrellabirds call similar to?

Vultures live on all continents except Antarctica and Australia. There are 23 species. Some vultures keep cool by peeing on their legs. This also disinfects them after feeding on a rotten carcass. Some vultures lack a voicebox, so grunt, hiss and clack their beaks to communicate.
Which vulture has the largest wingspan?

Wētā are New Zealand's most recognisable creepy-crawlies with their big bodies, spiny legs and curved tusks. Wētā are endemic to New Zealand with over 100 species spread over four groups. They are nocturnal and live in a variety of habitats: they're often found in gumboots!
Are wētā omnivores or herbivores?

X-ray tetra are a species of freshwater fish native to waterways in nothern South America and the Amazon region. They're also kept as pets in fish tanks. X-ray tetras love a diet of worms, insects and small crustaceans which live on the riverbed.
Why is it useful to be transparent?

Yellow-eyed penguins or hoiho are considered the rarest of the 18 species of penguin. They hunt offshore, diving to depths of up to 120 metres for food. Unlike other penguins which have dense colonies, hoiho prefer a bit of privacy and build their nests out of sight of each other.
Name a penguin that is also a type of pasta.

Zebu are one of the oldest breeds of cattle in the world. There are 75 different species of zebu. Their hump is a fat reservoir, which they use for energy when regular food is scarce. Millions of domesticated zebu can be found on farms throughout the world.
What is a young female zebu called?

Answers
A-aardvark B-pink D-yes E-green F-flamboyance G-humans H-hoglet I-active during the day J-4 knots K-brown, little spotted, great spotted, rowi, tokoeka L-cria M-omnivore N-numbats don't have a pouch, but use skin folds to cover their young O-torn P-lower teeth extend further than the upper teeth Q-covey, bevey or flock R-animal or plant that lives on or in another to survive S-kits T-yes U- hippopotamus V-condor W- omnivores X-hard for predators to see them Y-macaroni Z-heifer

Poetry Tips

Poetry is like painting a picture, but instead of using paint, you use words. Here are a few poetic devices (which is a fancy way of saying 'handy hints and tips') to make your poems the best they can be. Not all poems rhyme, not all poems have a set rhythm and not all poems have similes and metaphors – but all poems will paint you a picture using fabulous words.

Words

Writing poems, rhymes, ditties and limericks is fun. You get to play with words. Thinking of interesting and unusual words will make your poem even better. Use a thesaurus to find different words that mean a similar thing. For example, if you're writing about something 'big', try using 'humungous', 'colossal', or 'massive'. If you're describing the sound of bells, they do 'ring' but can also 'cling', 'clang', 'clong' and 'dong'. Have fun! Poems can be quite short, so make every word count.

Rhythm

Many poems have a rhythm, which helps make the words flow well. Rhythm is all about the syllables in each line – the beat. Clap your hands as you read your poem to make sure the beat or the rhythm is the same for each line.

Rhyme

A rhyme is a repetition of similar-sounding words, often at the ends of lines in poems. Many poems use rhymes and it's fun coming up with different and unusual rhymes. Check out 'Tt – tuatara' – every line ends with the same sound.

Alliteration

An easy way to make your poem sound even more like a poem is to use alliteration (when words that begin with the same letter are put next to or close to each other). Check out 'Bb – blobfish'– 'frightful, freaky, fish'.

Onomatopoeia

This is a long word for words that sound like what they mean. Onomatopoeia is fun to use in poems. Words like 'bang' and 'vroom' are examples. There are two examples in 'Oo – ocelot' – 'sniffly' and 'snuffly'.

Similes

Similes compare one thing with another thing by using the words 'as' or 'like'.

Check out 'Gg – gharial' – 'his teeth, as sharp as razors'.

Metaphors

Metaphors also compare, but as a statement rather than using 'as' or 'like'.

For example, 'My teacher is an angel'.

Personification

Personification is giving human qualities to objects, ideas or animals. For example, 'The moon smiled down on us'. The closest I get in this book is in 'Yy – yellow-eyed penguin', comparing them to humans dressed up in suits.

Format and punctuation

Poems don't look like a story. Stories go to the end of each line, and have paragraphs to break up the ideas. Poems can be short and fat, or long and skinny, or even in the shape of something. Make your poem look like a poem; make it look interesting. The way you break up the lines will make the person read it the way you want it to sound. Your punctuation will also make the reader slow down or speed up. Check out the long and thin 'Uu – umbrellabird'.

Repetition

Repetition can help the rhythm of a poem, help emphasise ideas, and is fun to do.

Check out 'Hh – hedgehog'.

Limericks

Limericks always have the same rhythm, and are often funny. The first two lines and the fifth line have the same number of syllables, and the second and third lines have an equal number of syllables. Check out 'Kk – kiwi'.

AND, MOST IMPORTANTLY ... HAVE FUN!

For Alex, Mum and my delightful children, and with huge thanks to Deborah for bringing all the weird and wonderful animals to life so very beautifully – Jo

For Tai and Jayda who both love unusual animals – DH

A catalogue record of this book is available from the National Library of New Zealand.

ISBN: 978-0-473-58084-1

A PictureBook Publishing publication.
Published in 2021 by PictureBook Publishing
PO Box 455 Te Awamutu 3840 New Zealand.
www.picturebook.co.nz

Text © Jo van Dam, 2021
Illustrations © Deborah Hinde 2021.

Book design by Deborah Hinde
www.deborahhinde.co.nz
Edited by Sue Copsey www.suecopsey.com
Printed in China by 1010 Printing Ltd